I'm Done!

by GRETCHEN BRANDENBURG McLELLAN

illustrated by CATHERINE LAZAR ODELL

Holiday House New York

To Judi, Carol, Ellen, Karen, and Sue,
    writing group extraordinaire —G.M.   To Jack and Grandmother —C.O.

HOLIDAY HOUSE is registered in the U.S. Patent and Trademark Office.
Printed and Bound in May 2018 at Tien Wah Press, Johor Bahru, Johor, Malaysia.
www.holidayhouse.com
First Edition
1 3 5 7 9 10 8 6 4 2

Library of Congress Cataloging-in-Publication Data

Names: McLellan, Gretchen Brandenburg, author. | Odell, Catherine, illustrator.
Title: I'm done! / by Gretchen Brandenburg McLellan ; illustrated by Catherine Odell.
Other titles: I am done!
Description: First edition. | [New York] : Holiday House, [2018] |
Summary: Little Beaver would rather play with friends than build a proper dam, but
finally he is ready to get it done.
Identifiers: LCCN 2017024829 | ISBN 9780823437054 (hardcover)
Subjects: | CYAC: Beavers—Fiction. | Dams—Fiction. | Perseverance (Ethics)—Fiction. | Friendship—Fiction.
Classification: LCC PZ7.1.M4627 Im 2018 | DDC [E]—dc23 LC record available
at https://lccn.loc.gov/2017024829

Nibble Nibble Snap

Little Beaver carried a twig to the stream.
He set it across the water.
"I'M DONE!" he called to Mama and Papa.

Flish Flish Swish

It was Fish!

"Bet you can't catch me," Fish said.
Little Beaver followed Fish

splish, splish, splash

down the stream.

SLAP! SLAP! SLAP!

Papa's tail slapped the water.

Little Beaver scurried back.
"You're done?" Papa asked.
Little Beaver nodded.
"Not yet," Papa said.

Nibble Nibble Snap

Nibble Nibble Snap

Little Beaver dragged two more sticks to the stream and set them across the water. **"I'M DONE!"** he called.

Wing Wing Zing

Blue feathers flashed high above.

"Bet you can't find me!" Bird said.

Little Beaver followed Bird
wiggle, wiggle, waddle
through the trees.

SLAP! SLAP! SLAP!

Mama's tail slapped the water.
Little Beaver hurried back.
"You're done?" Mama asked.
He nodded.

"Little Beaver, what are your paws for?"
"Paddling and playing and—patting."
"And scooping," Mama said. "You're not
done yet."

Nibble   Nibble   Snap

Nibble   Nibble   Snap

Nibble   Nibble   Snap

Little Beaver set
three more branches
across the water.

Scoop   Scoop   Pat
        Scoop   Scoop   Pat

He patty-caked them
together with mud.
"I'M DONE!" he called.

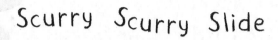

Scurry Scurry Slide

Otter scooted by.
"Bet you can't tag me!" Otter said.
Little Beaver chased Otter into the big pond.

Twirl Twirl Swirl

He whirled down deep and
tagged Otter. "You're it!"

SLAP! SLAP! SLAP!

Papa's tail smacked the water.
Uh-oh!

Little Beaver paddled to Papa.
"Follow me," Papa said.
Little Beaver trailed Papa back to
his pile of twigs and mud.

"Little Beaver, what is a dam for?" Papa asked.
"Making a pond."
"Where is your pond?"
Little Beaver looked under a leaf. Papa didn't smile.
"You're not done yet, are you?"

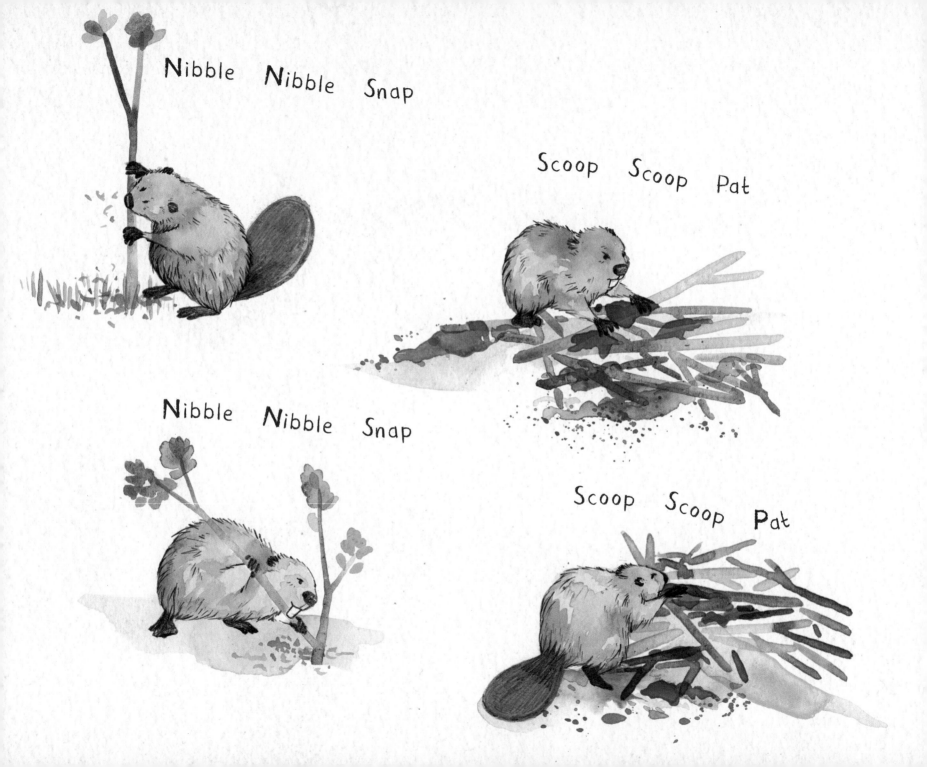

Nibble Nibble Snap

Scoop Scoop Pat

Nibble Nibble Snap

Scoop Scoop Pat

Nibble Nibble Snap

Scoop Scoop Pat

"I'M DONE!" Little Beaver said.

But Papa was working on their family dam, and
Mama was working on their lodge. Two busy,
too busy to come.

So Little Beaver carried a branch to help Papa.

"I'M DONE!"

"We'll see," Papa said.
Little Beaver paddled a branch to Mama.

"I'M DONE!"

"We'll see. Later," she said. "Right now
it's time for bed."

In their cozy den Mama sang a
song of a busy little beaver
whose dam was nearly done.

Little Beaver dreamed of

nibble nibble snap,   scoop scoop pat,

slap slap slap.

Whoosh!
The sound of water rushing through his dam startled Little Beaver awake. He hurried outside.

There was still work to do.

Nibble Nibble Snap

Scoop Scoop Pat

The sun dipped and Bird called for him to race.
"Not yet!" Little Beaver said.
So Bird stayed to help.

Nibble Nibble Snap

Scoop Scoop Pat

The moon rose and Otter called
for him to chase.
"Not yet!" Little Beaver said.
So Otter stayed to help.

Nibble Nibble Snap   Scoop Scoop Pat

Fireflies glowed and Fish called
for him to swim.
"Not yet!" Little Beaver said.
So Fish helped too.

Nibble Nibble Snap

Scoop Scoop Pat

Pat Pat Pat—

Oh!
Little Beaver and his friends watched in
wonder as silvery water pooled behind his dam.
He waded into his pond and lifted his tail.

SLAP! SLAP! SLAP!

His tail smacked the shiny water.

"Mama! Papa!" he called. **"I'M REALLY DONE!"**

Mama and Papa scurried to his side.
"Oh, Little Beaver! You really are done!"
"HOORAY!" everyone cheered.

Little Beaver turned to his friends.
"Now?" asked Bird.
"Now?" asked Otter.
"Now?" asked Fish.
"NOW!" Little Beaver said with a slap
of his tail. "Race you across my pond!"

And wing, paddle, zing—
they did!